" …and the Big Bad Wolf huffed and puffed all the way home."

It's the same old story. Wolves are crusty, lazy, and mean.
They howl, they chase, and they make a mess.
We know all about big bad wolves and their nasty ways…

Don't we?

crumbs

Grub

Hairball

Scribble

Knits

Yoyo

First edition for the United States, its territories and dependencies, and Canada published in 2006 by Barron's Educational Series, Inc.

First published by Hodder Children's Books, a division of Hodder Headline Limited
338 Euston Road
London NW1 3BH

All inquiries should be addressed to:
Barron's Educational Series, Inc.
250 Wireless Boulevard
Hauppauge, NY 11788
www.barronseduc.com

ISBN-13: 978-0-7641-5991-6
ISBN-10: 0-7641-5991-7

Library of Congress Control Number: 2005936624

Printed in China
9 8 7 6 5 4 3 2 1

For Marianne, Alex, Rosie, and Daniel.

Love to Monika and Luka and a thank you
to Igor who patiently drove me to the four corners
of Dugo Selo.

Plus a special thank you to Geraldine Stroud.

THE SCALLYWAGS

Jumble

Earwax

Brooz

David Melling

BARRON'S

It was a full moon and the Scallywags were late, **again**.
The other animals had arrived early and were dressed in their best.
But now the photographer was tapping his watch.

"We can wait no longer," he complained,
"or the beautiful silver light will be
gone and the picture will be ruined!"

He looked into the lens one last time.
"Say **cheese** everyone."

"Cheeeeese!"

"CRASH!" "BANG!" "WALLOP!"

The wolves smashed into the camera, the photographer, and the other animals.

"You hairy **nincompoops!**" yelled the photographer.

"Typical wolves," mumbled the others.

The next morning, the animals gathered around to see the photograph. They were so mad that they decided not to ask the wolves to eat breakfast with them.

"They'll just **spoil** it for everyone," said the moose.

"I agree," said a bear. "They always *throw* the food and nibble on the napkins!"

"I sat next to one of them at supper time last week," said a pig.
"He was SO *smelly,* I couldn't finish eating!"

Meanwhile, the wolves were wasting time at home.

Jumble, the leader of the Scallywags, gave his tummy a poke.

"I'm hungry," he said. "What time is breakfast?"

"Dunno," said Earwax, "but I can smell it!"

The pack wagged their scratchy tails, pointed their twitchy noses, and trotted after the delicious smells.

But when they arrived, the other animals had already finished.

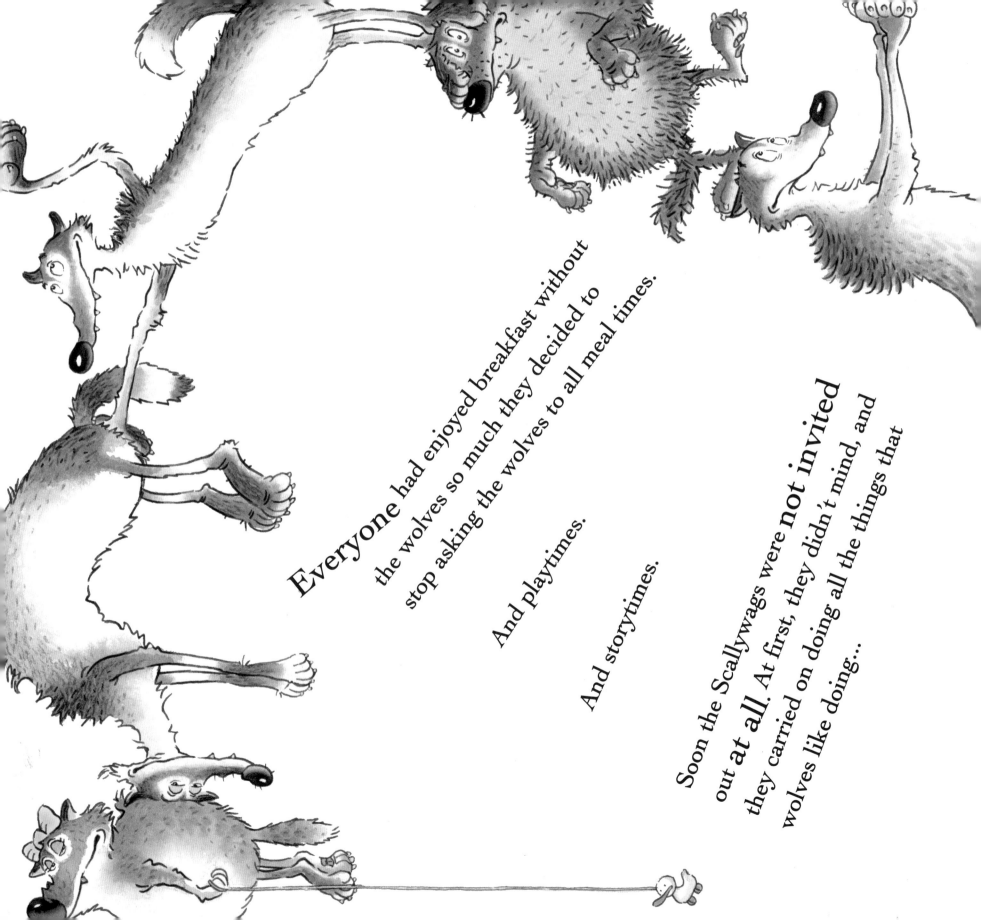

Everyone had enjoyed breakfast without the wolves so much they decided to stop asking the wolves to all meal times.

And playtimes.

And storytimes.

Soon the Scallywags were not invited out at all. At first, they didn't mind, and they carried on doing all the things that wolves like doing...

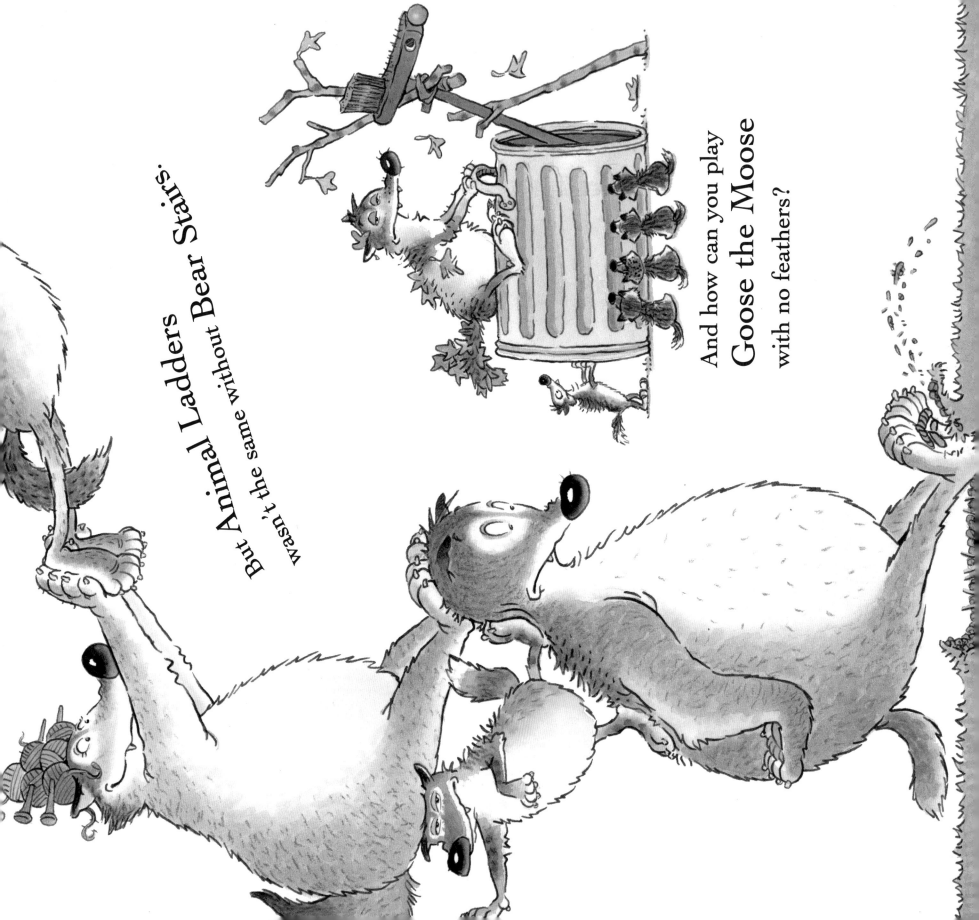

But **Animal Ladders**
wasn't the same without **Bear Stairs**.

And how can you play
Goose the Moose with no feathers?

"What we have to do is show everyone that we aren't so bad," said Jumble.

"Yeah," said Brooz, "no one gets to see our soft and cuddly side."

"Maybe if we had better manners!" coughed Hairball.

"But we don't got no manners," said Scribble.

YoYo sniffed his armpit. "I suppose we could take a bath."

"And I could make some nice clothes," said Knits.

Jumble sat up—"I know, let's go into town, follow the other animals around, and copy what they do. Then they're bound to like us!"

So, every day, the Scallywags snooped and spied with their big eyes!

And every night they practiced **very hard**.

Before long **most** of the wolves knew what to do with…

a handkerchief,

a toothbrush,

and a comb.

And **some** of them could dress nicely and say *please* and thank you.

And so came the day when the Scallywags decided to visit
the other animals and show them how much fun wolves can be!

The animals were happy to see nine neat visitors dressed
in clothes that shined.

They didn't recognize the Scallywags and
asked the wolves to stay for a bite to eat.

But no sooner had the soup arrived
than the **trouble** began.

Scribble leaned across to one of the pigs and smiled sweetly.

"Excuse me," he said, "please don't slurp your soup, it makes a breeze. Thank you so much!"

It didn't stop there. The wolves checked that all the animals had washed their hands, paws, feet, and claws.

They told the geese not to **honk** with their beaks full, and a family of bears were reminded not to leave the table until everybody had finished.

The animals soon changed their minds about the fussy guests and began to realize how much they missed the Scallywags.

"Of course the wolves are noisy," they whispered, "but at least they're funny, and they can enjoy themselves without telling **everybody else** what to do!"

Above them the moon came out. A full moon.

The wolves became restless —they loosened their buttons.
They started to itch and they started to scratch.

Grub pressed his elbows into a sandwich… on purpose.

Scribble giggled.

Crumbs bit YoYo's toe.

Earwax squashed a pea on Jumble's nose.

Hairball's tail pop^ped out and
Knits chewed on it. Hairball yelled.

Brooz howled. They all howwled.

"The Scallywags!" gasped the animals.

For a minute nobody moved. Then Jumble coughed—
"Would anyone like a sandwich?"

"Yes please!" they said and they all dug in!

The animals were so busy enjoying themselves that they forgot to
be angry with the wolves. And the wolves forgot… well, everything!

The photographer smiled and set up his camera. "Ready everyone?"

"Cheeeeese!"